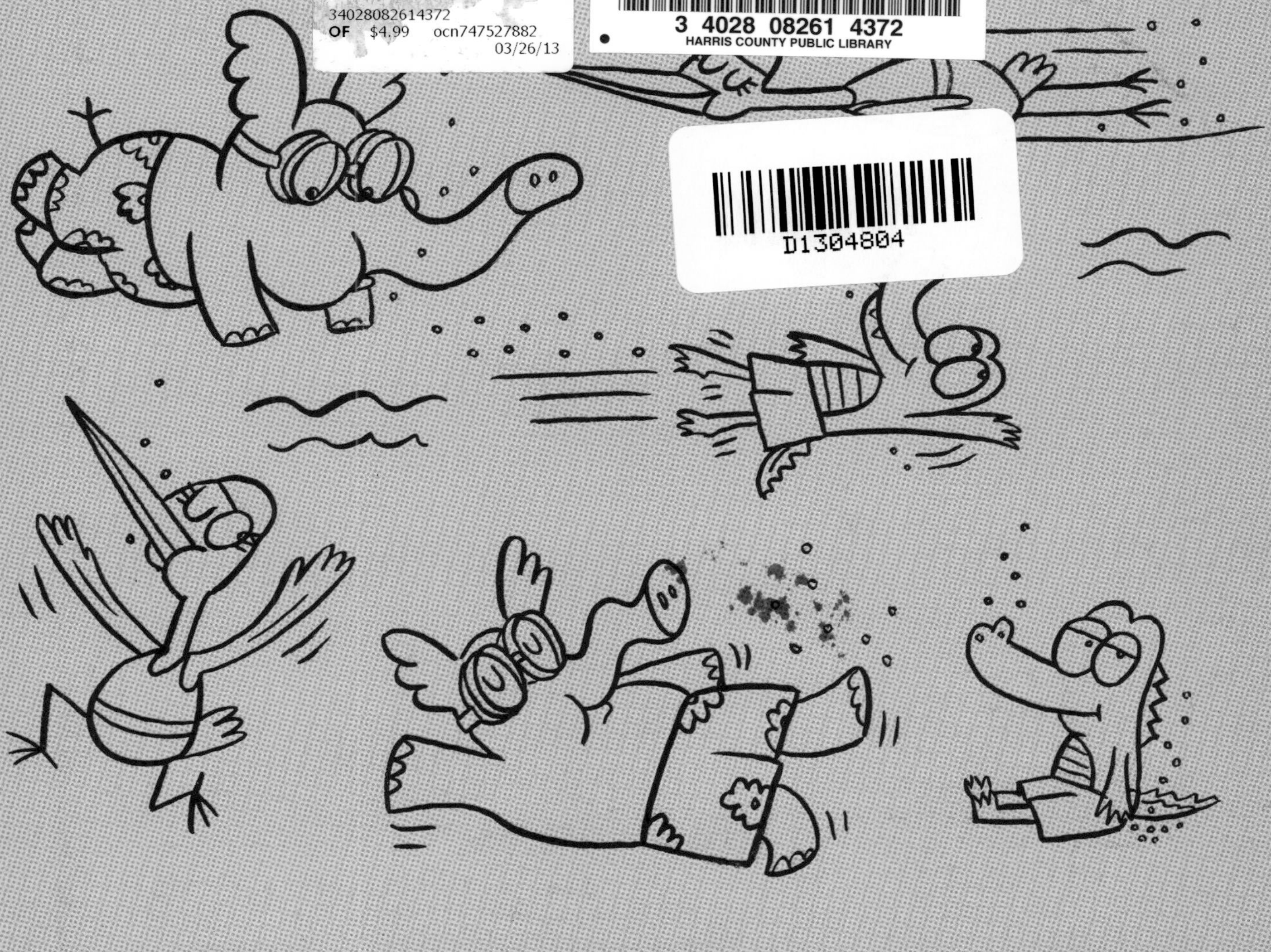

Copyright © 2012 Ethan Long

Balloon Toons® is a registered trademark of Harriet Ziefert, Inc.

All rights reserved/CIP data is available. Published in the United States 2012 by

Blue Apple Books, 515 Valley Street, Maplewood, NJ 07040

www.blueapplebooks.com

First Edition   Printed in China 03/12

HC ISBN: 978-1-60905-201-0   PB ISBN: 978-1-60905-202-7

1 2 3 4 5 6 7 8 9 10   1 2 3 4 5 6 7 8 9 10

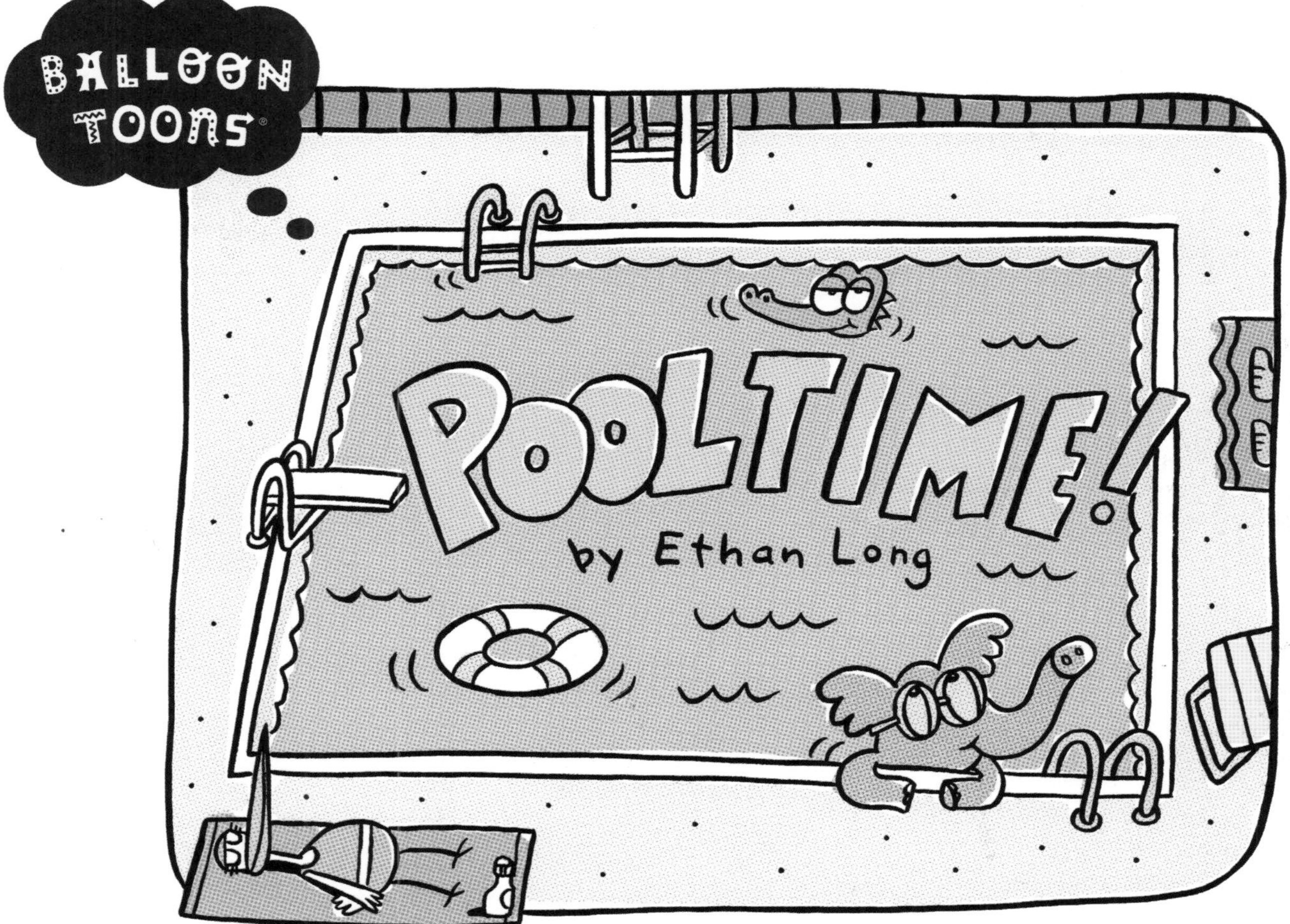
BALLOON TOONS®
POOLTIME!
by Ethan Long

BLUE APPLE

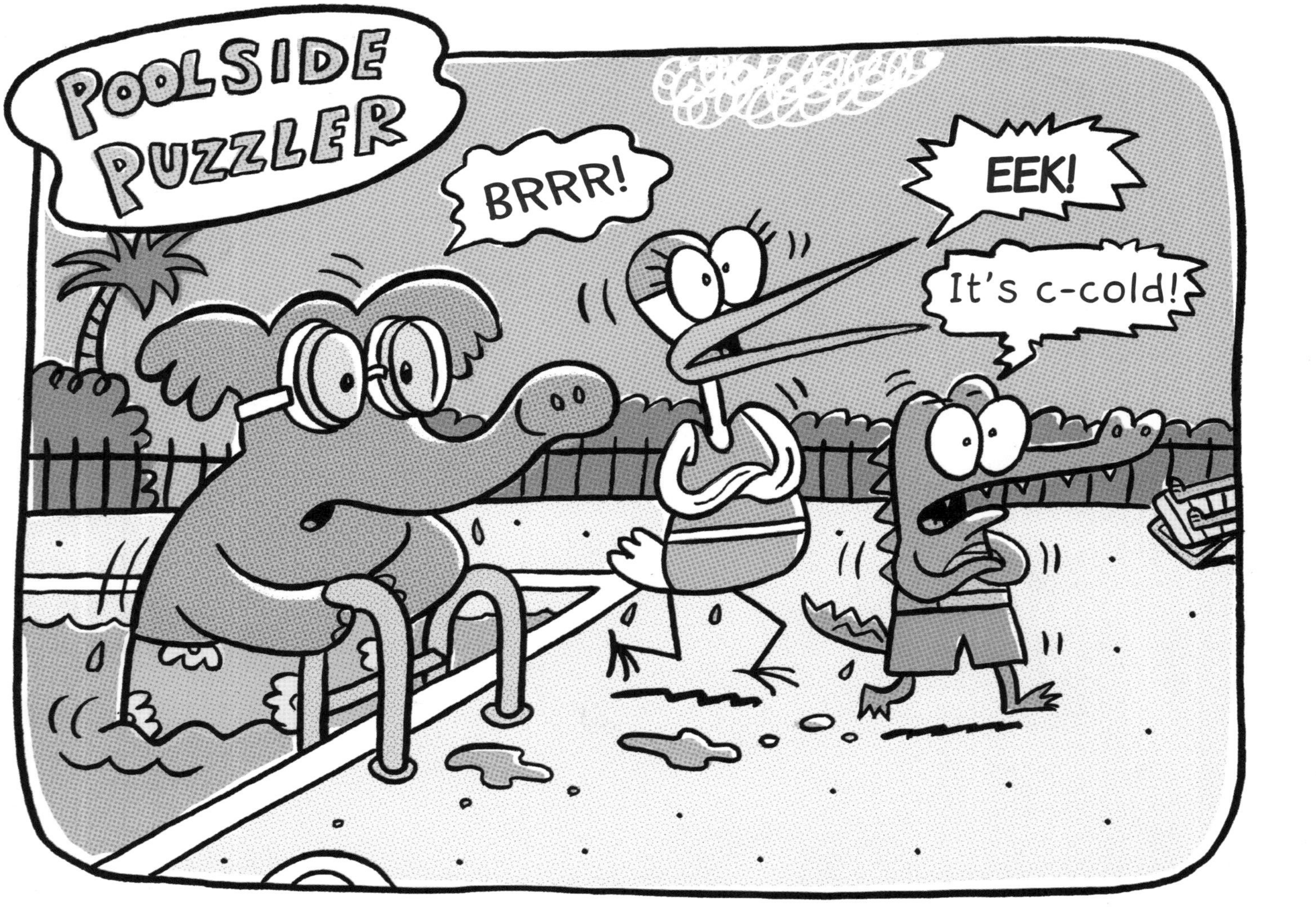
POOLSIDE PUZZLER
BRRRR!
EEK!
It's c-cold!

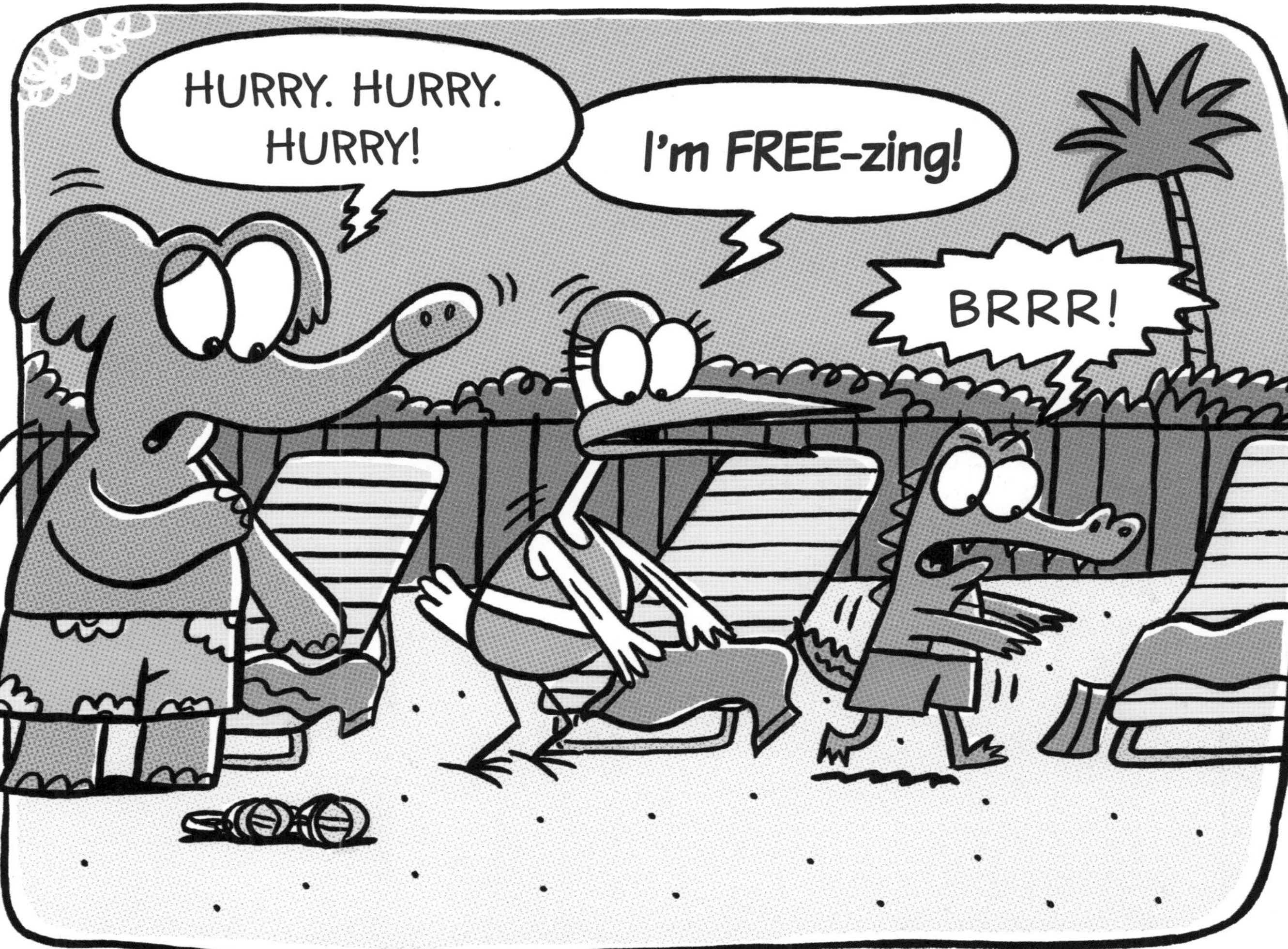
HURRY. HURRY. HURRY!
I'm FREE-zing!
BRRR!

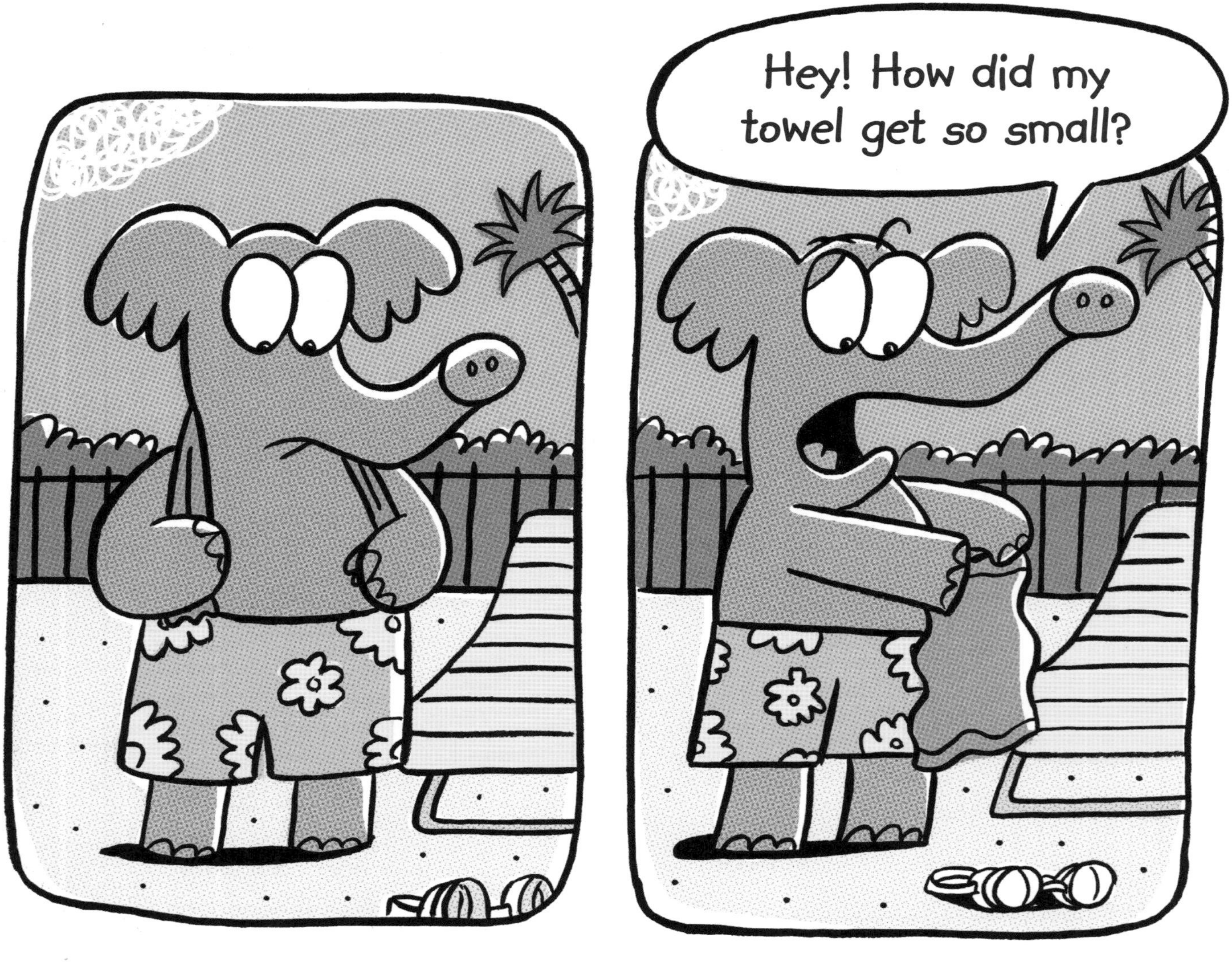
Hey! How did my towel get so small?

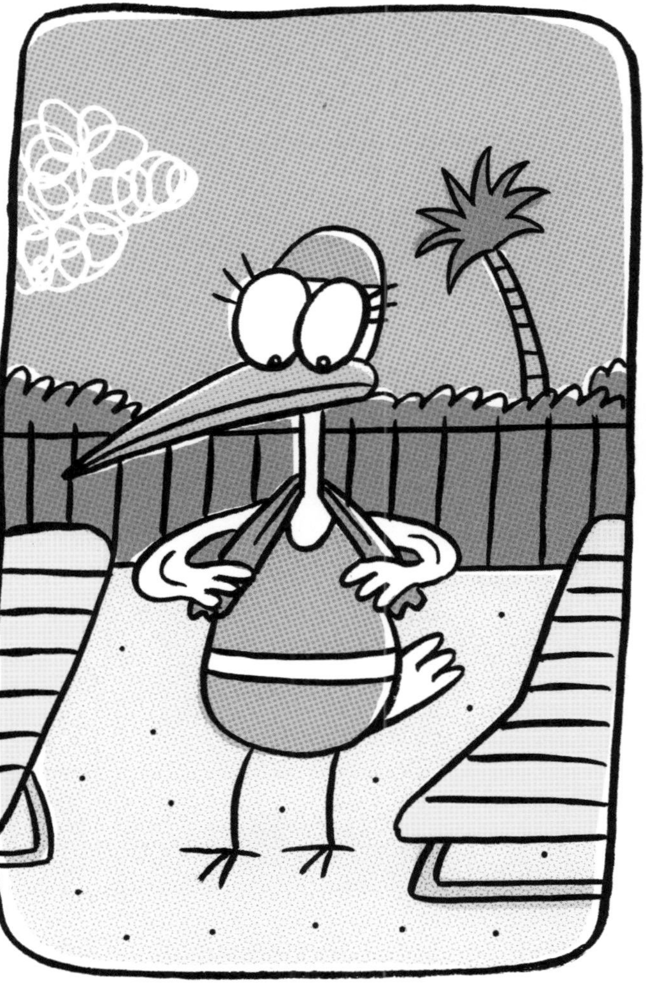

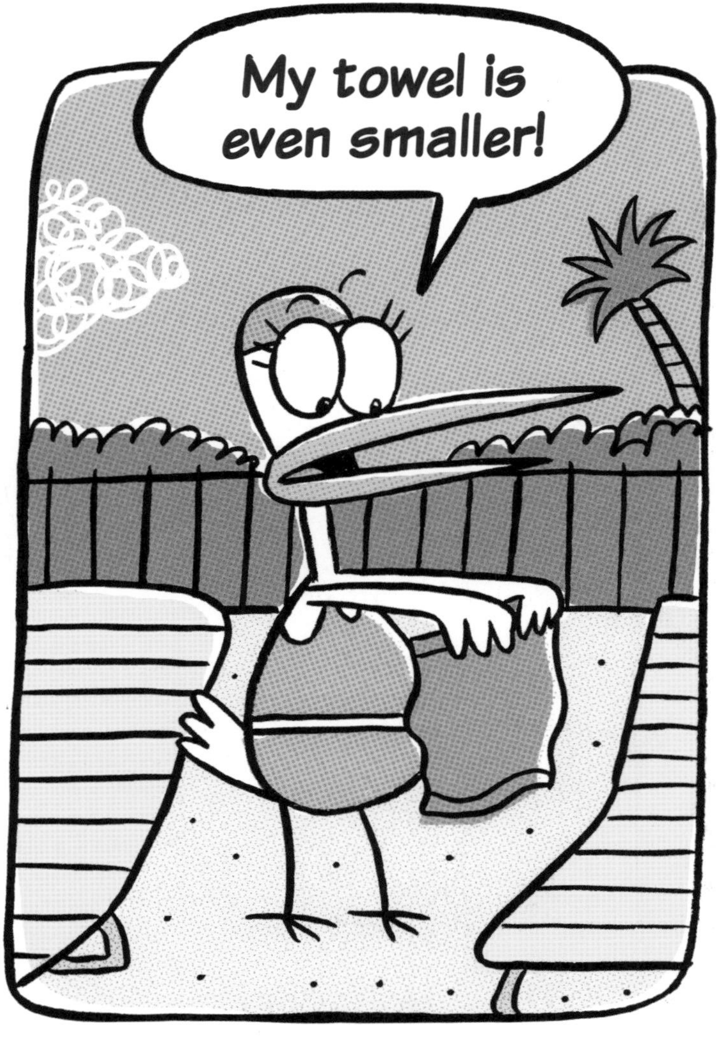
My towel is even smaller!

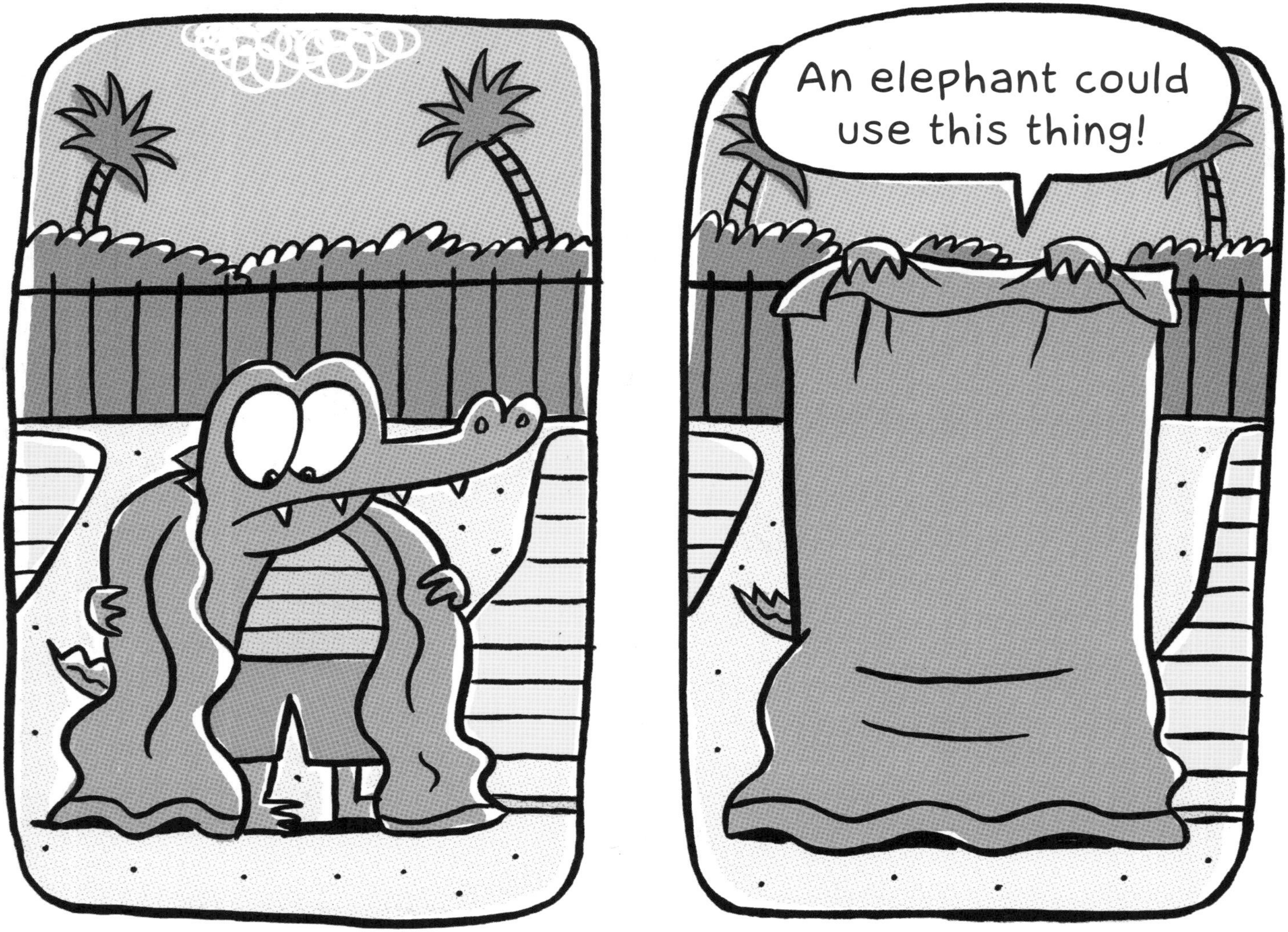
An elephant could use this thing!

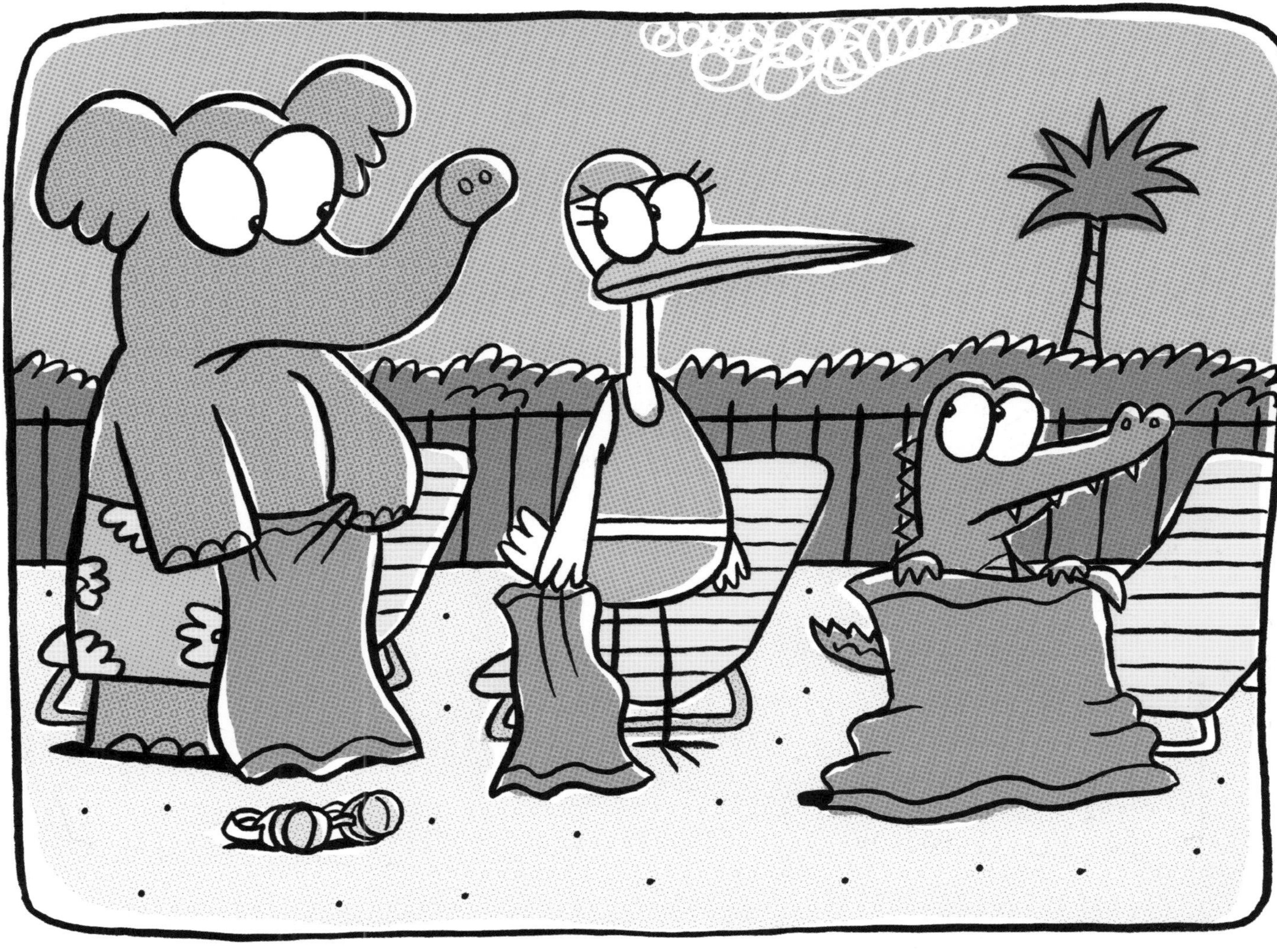

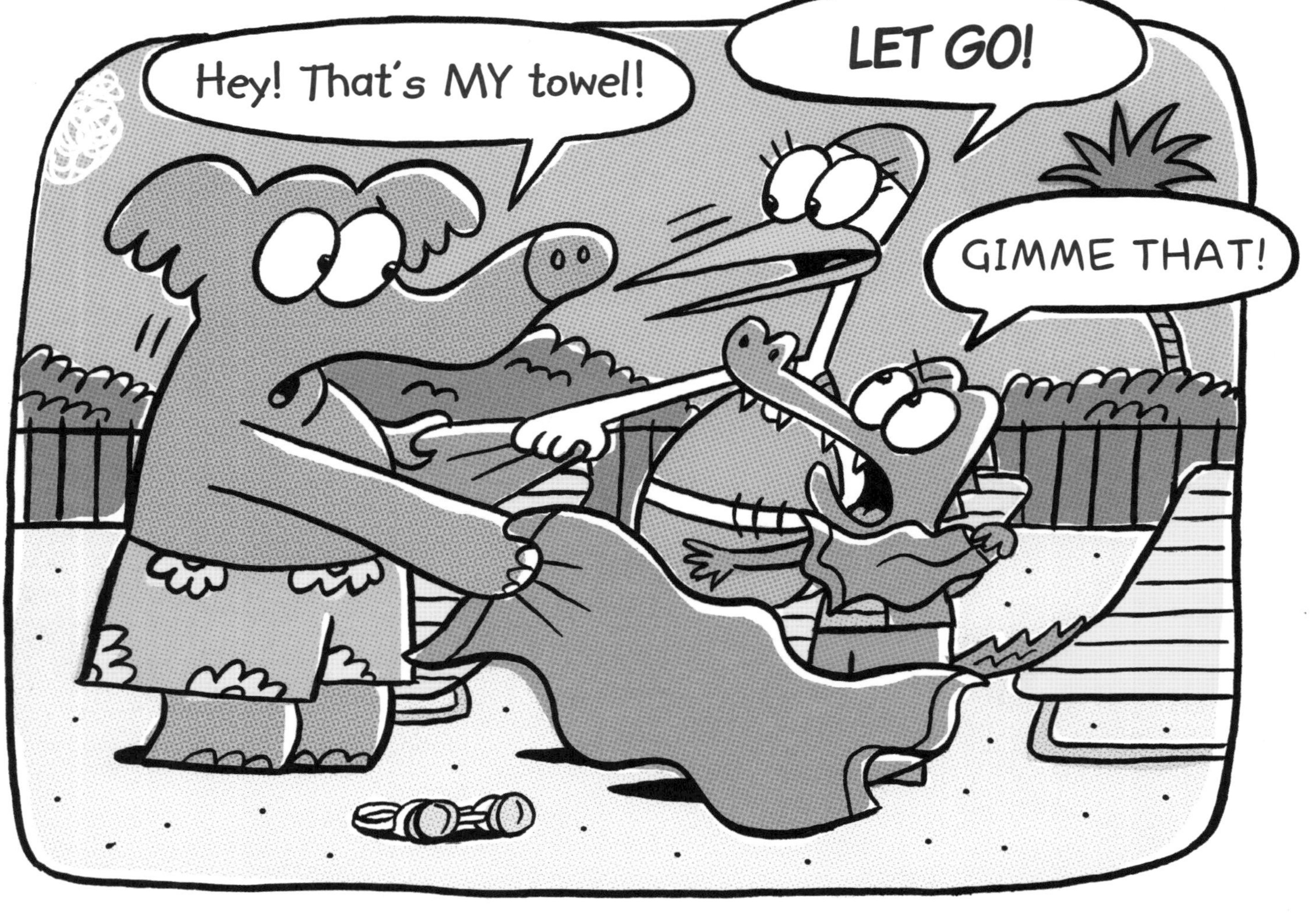
Hey! That's MY towel!
LET GO!
GIMME THAT!

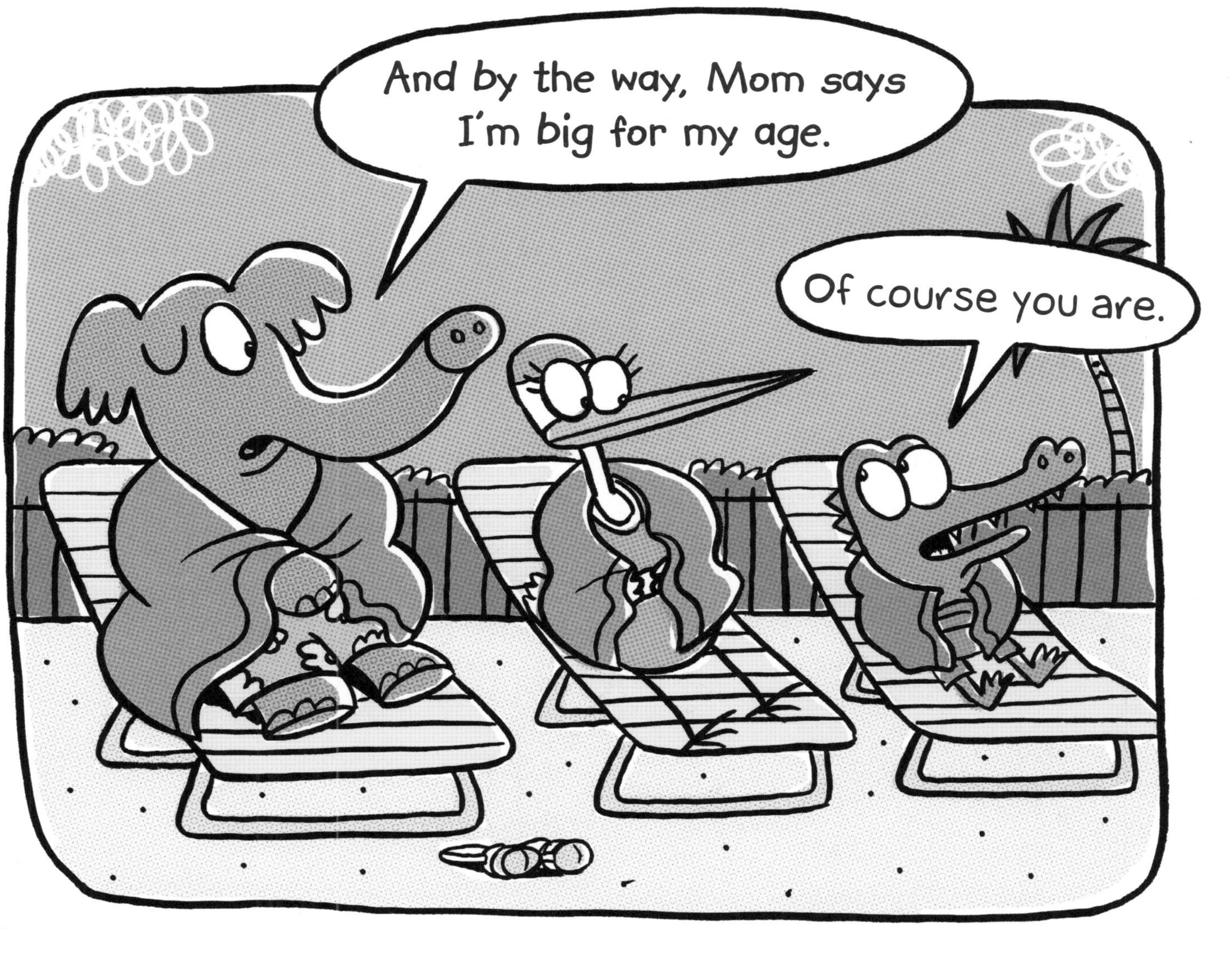
And by the way, Mom says I'm big for my age.
Of course you are.

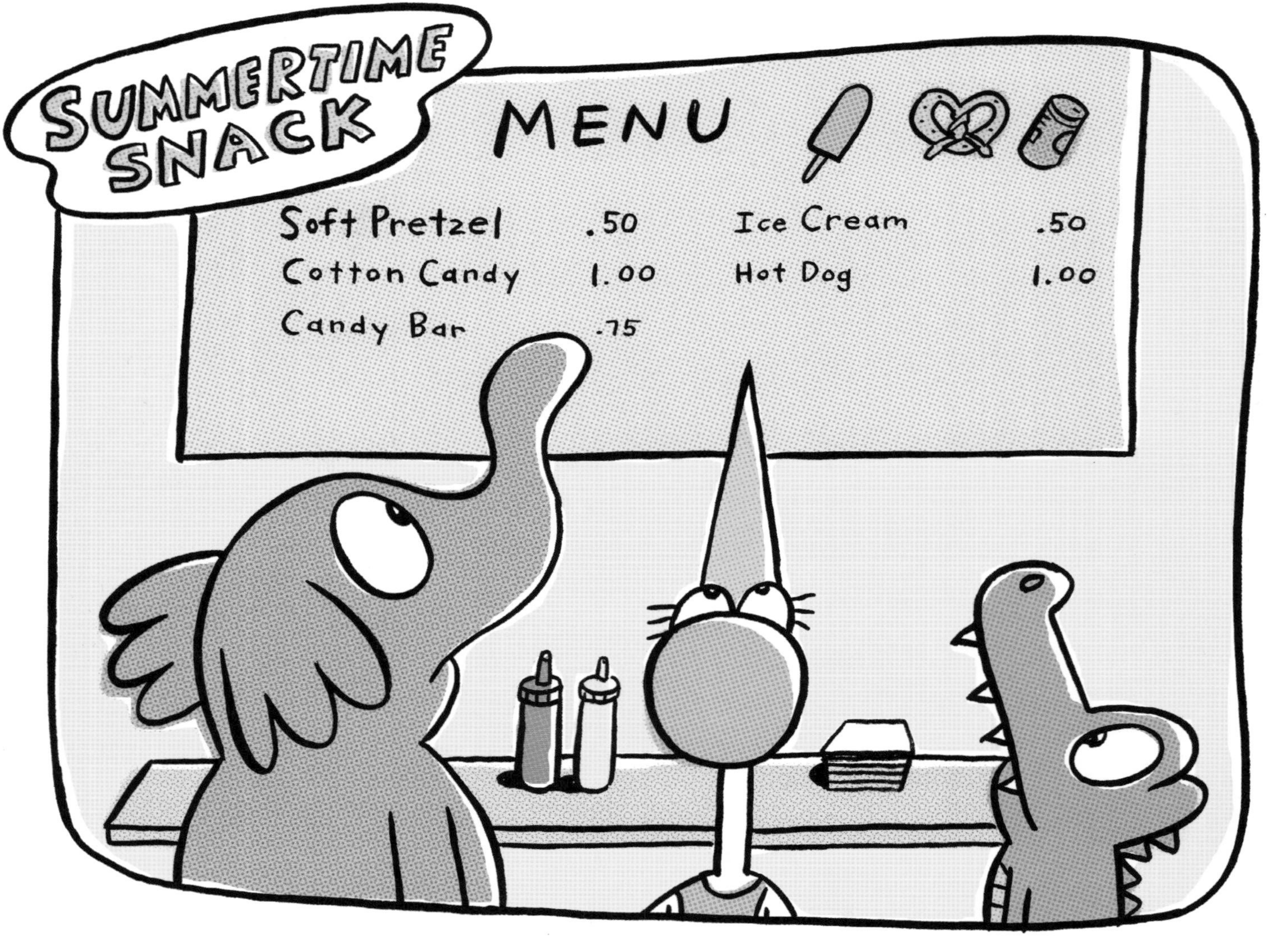
SUMMERTIME SNACK
MENU
Soft Pretzel .50
Cotton Candy 1.00
Candy Bar .75
Ice Cream .50
Hot Dog 1.00

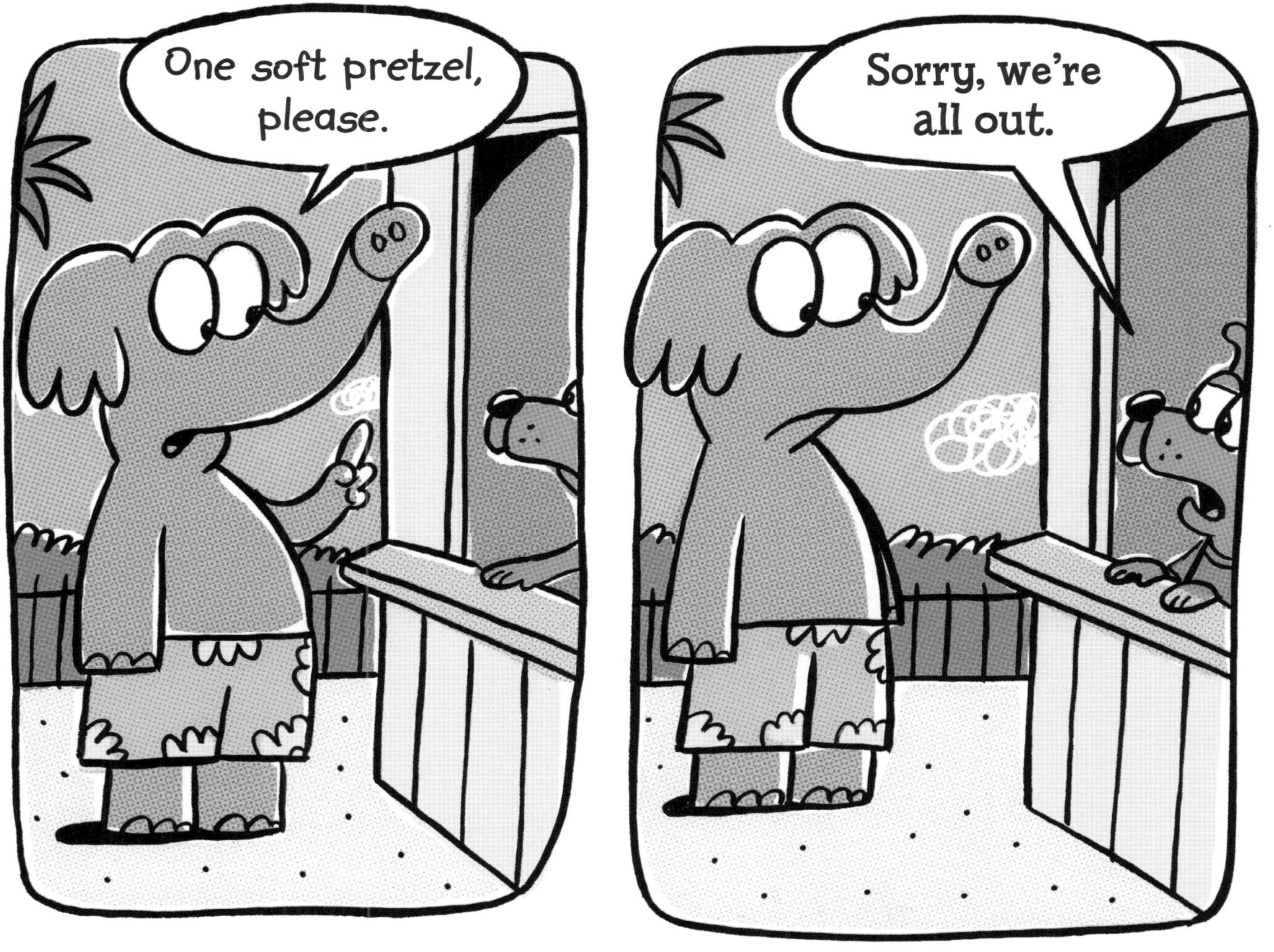
One soft pretzel, please.
Sorry, we're all out.

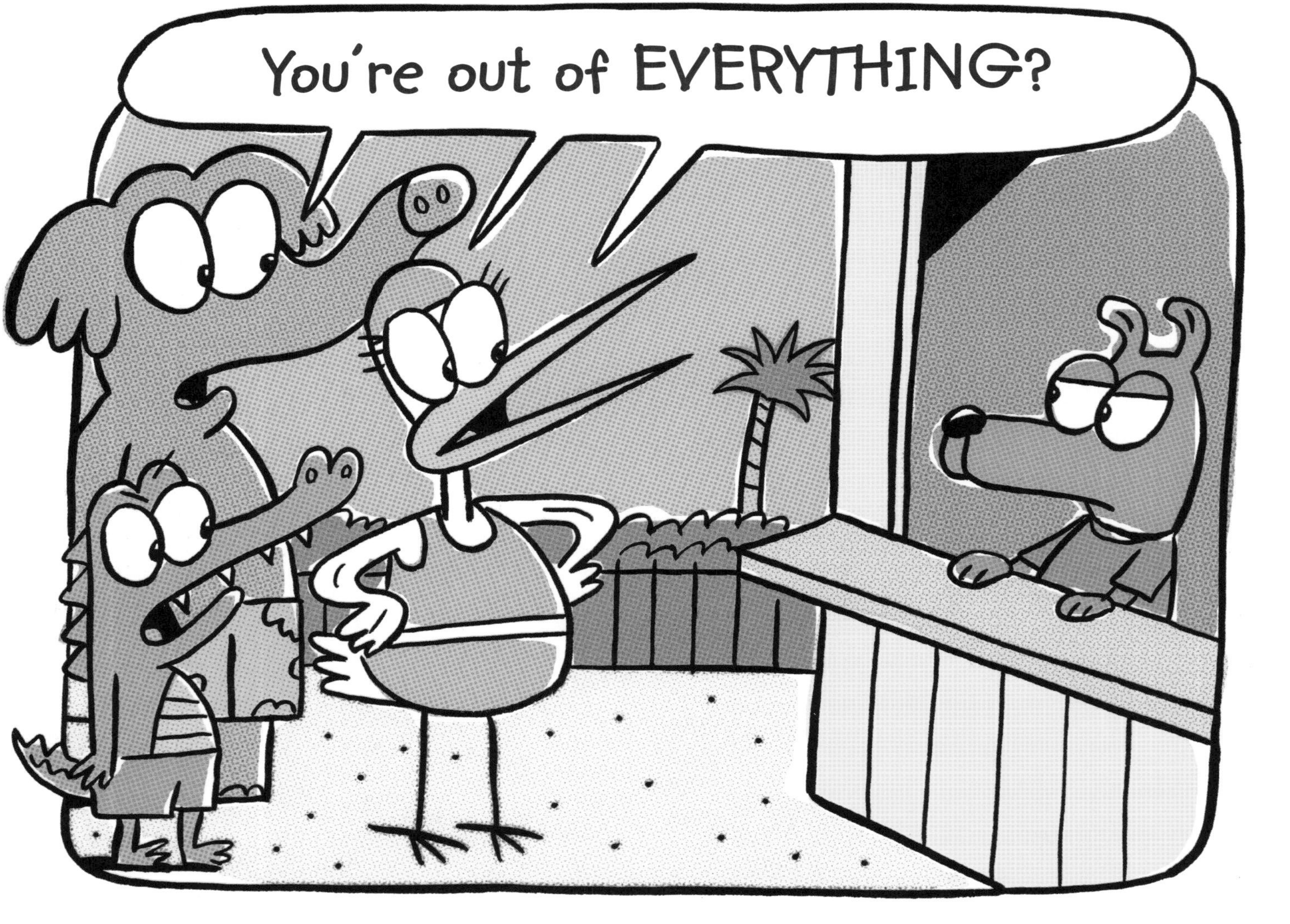
You're out of EVERYTHING?

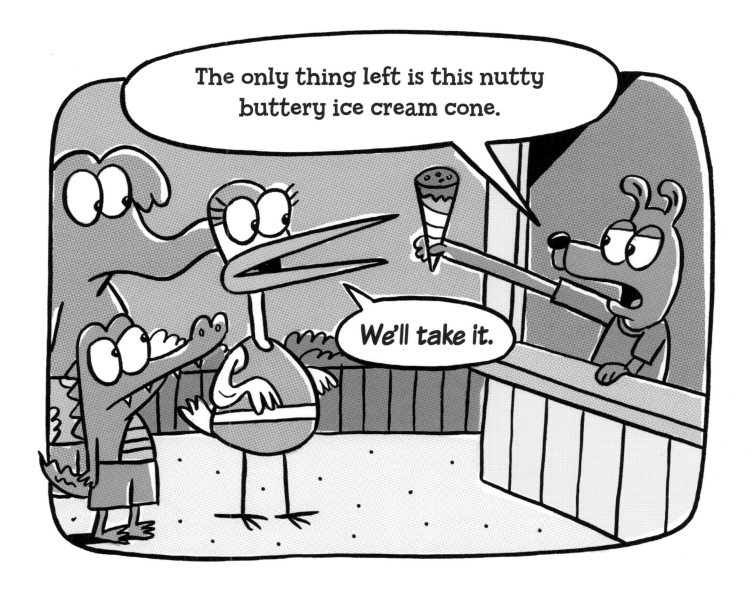

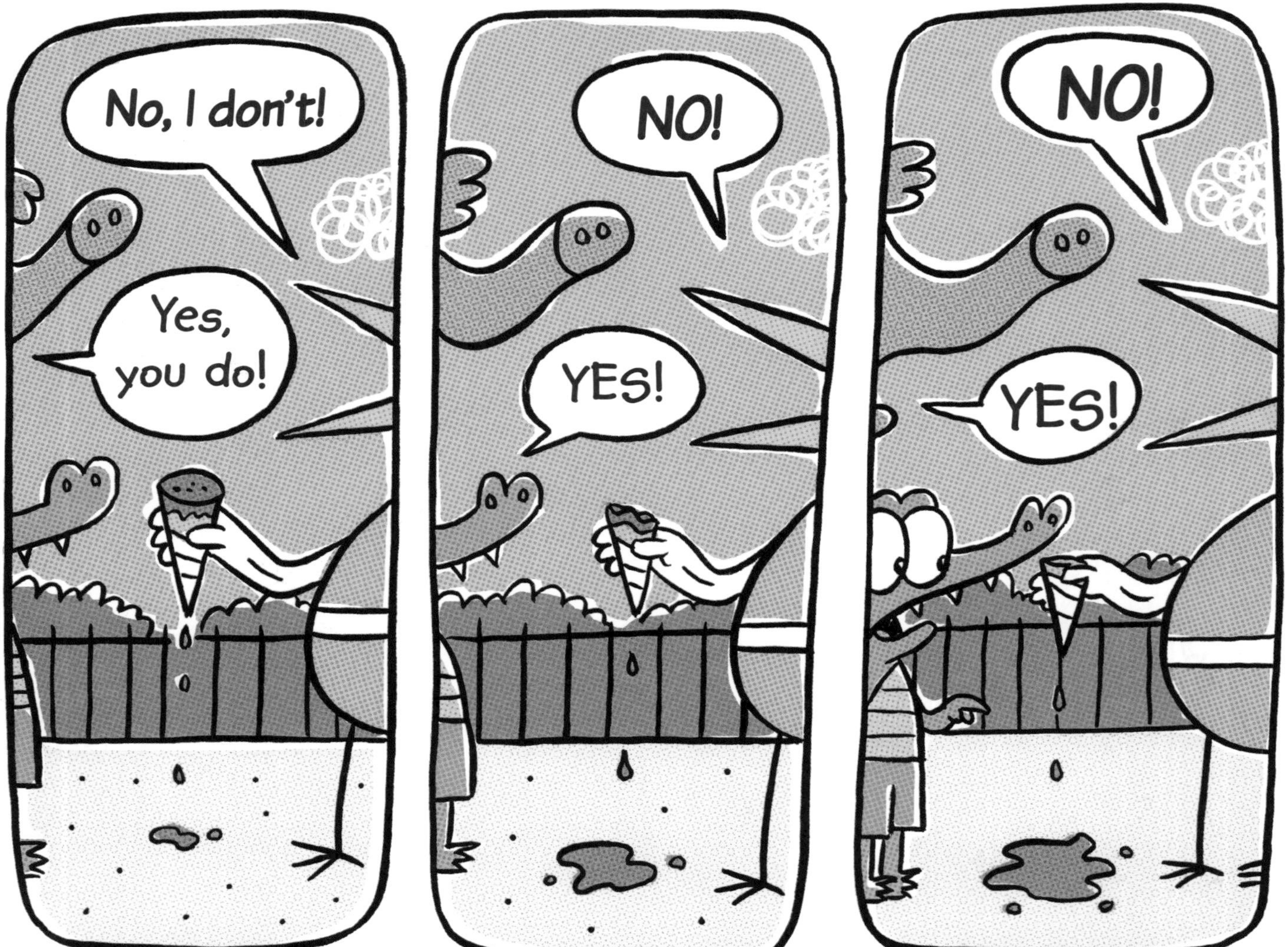
No, I don't!
Yes, you do!
NO!
YES!
NO!
YES!

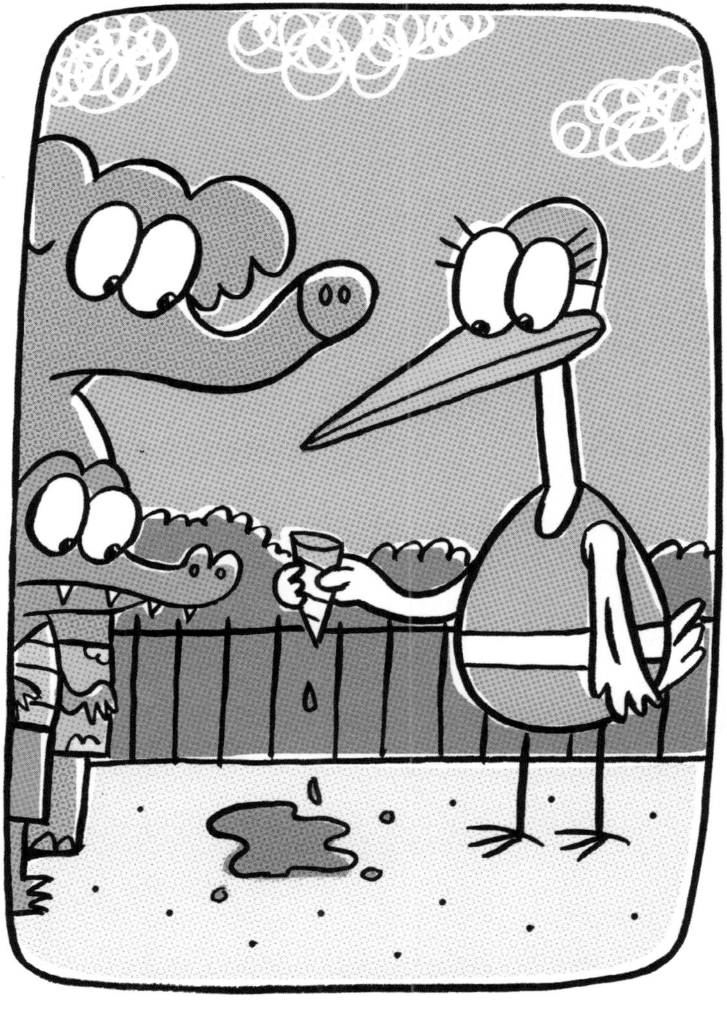

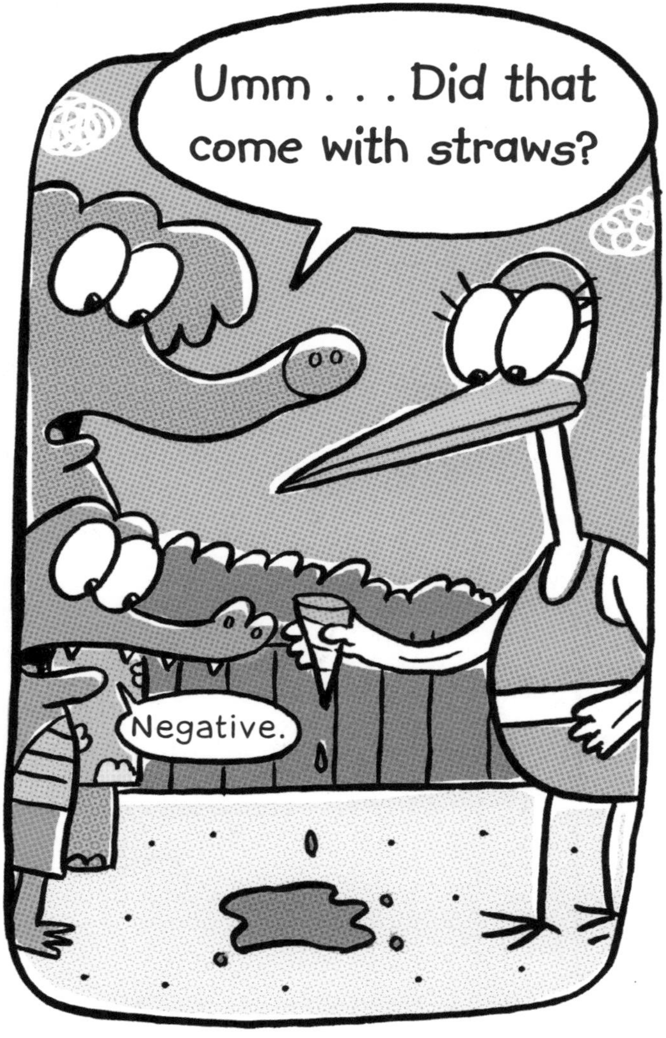
Umm . . . Did that come with straws?
Negative.

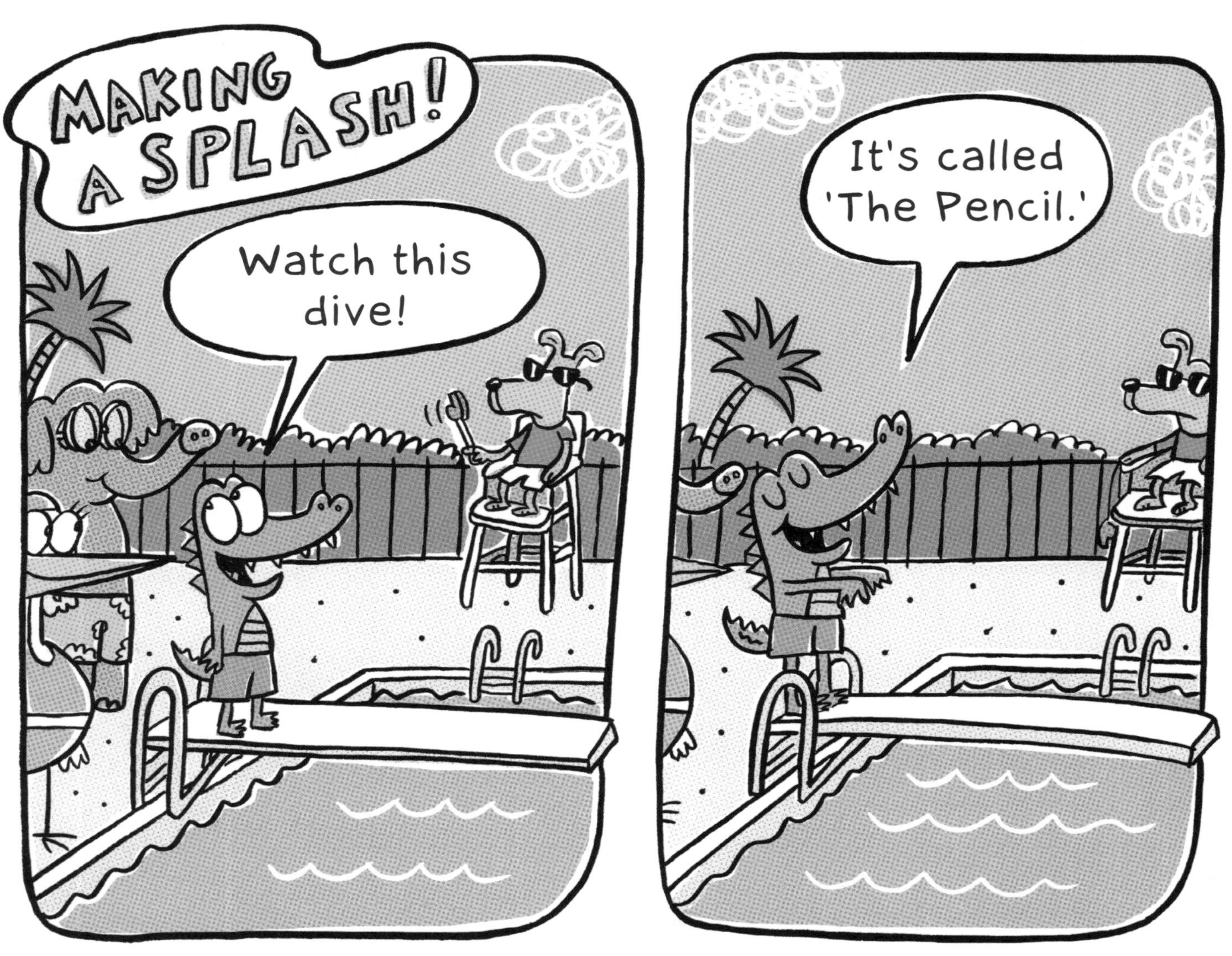
MAKING A SPLASH!
Watch this dive!
It's called 'The Pencil.'

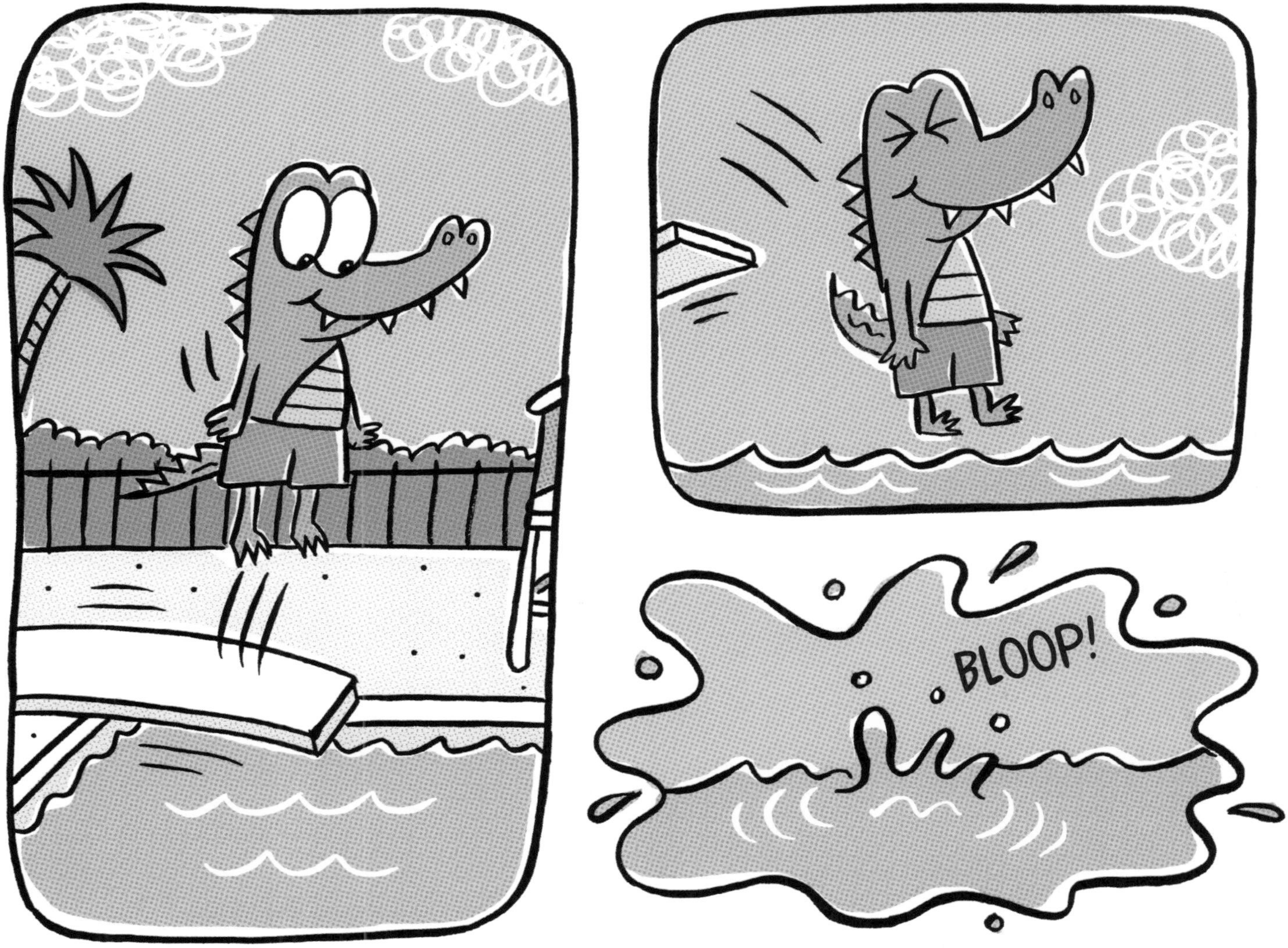
BLOOP!

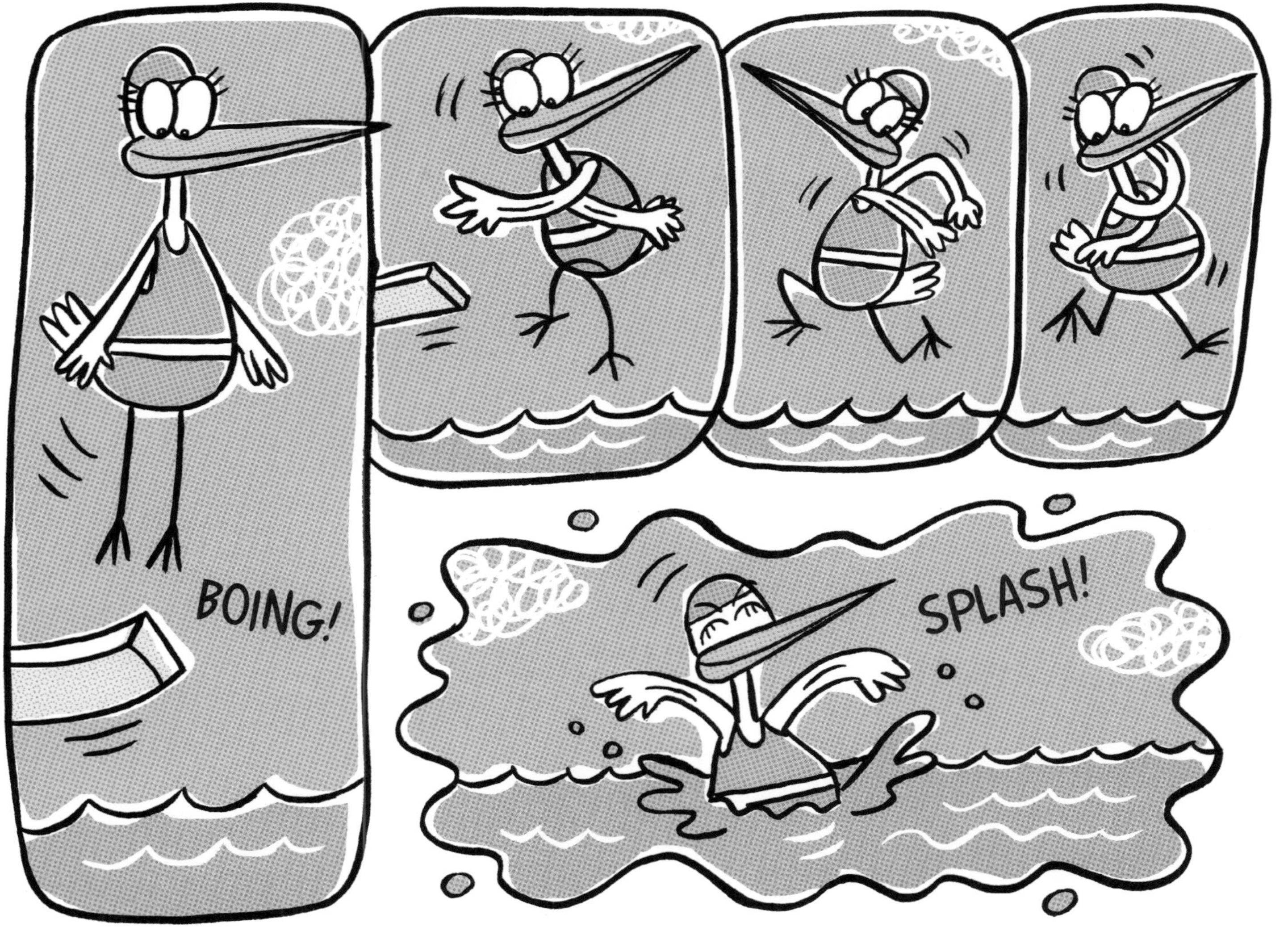
BOING!
SPLASH!

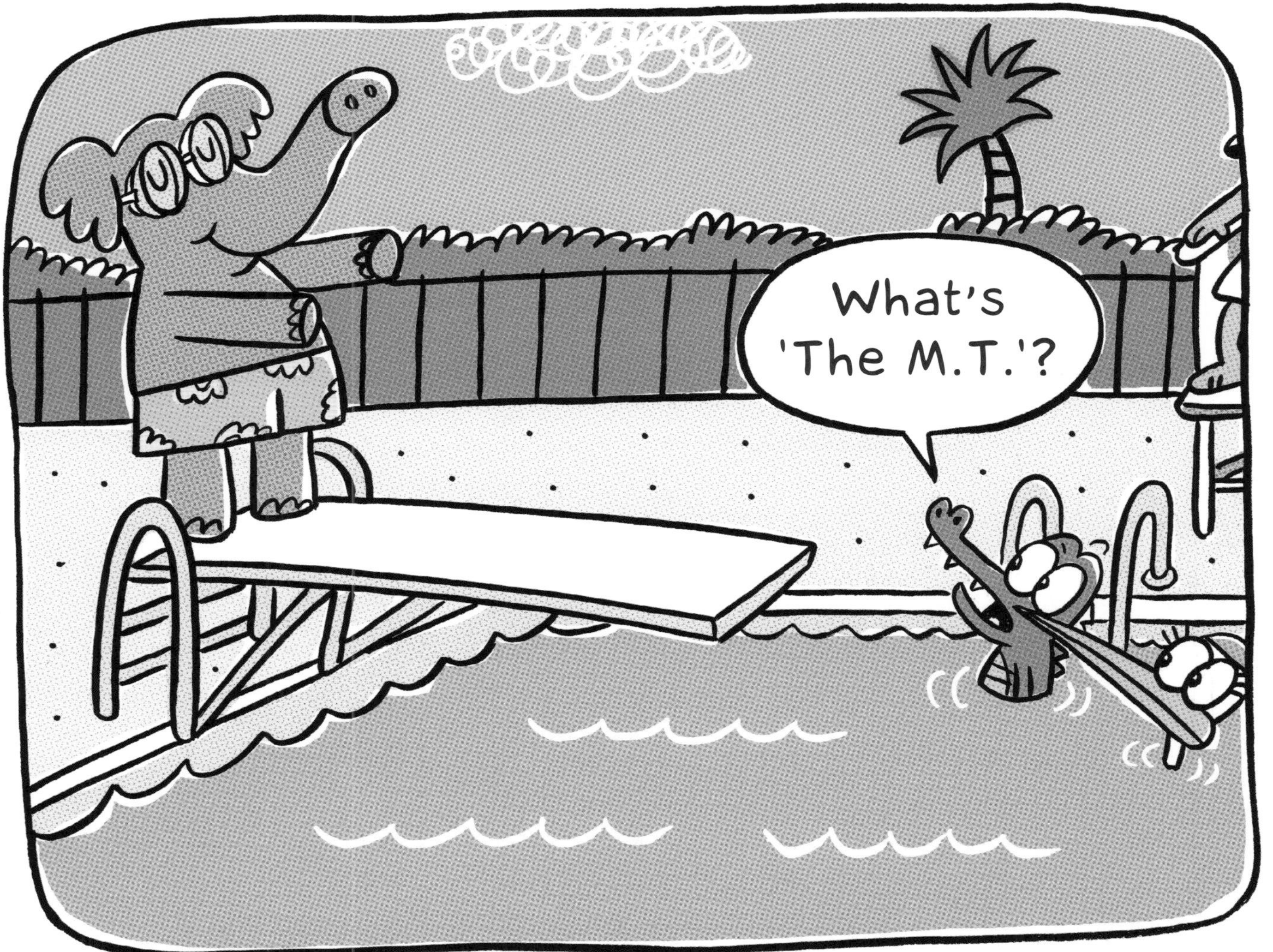
What's 'The M.T.'?

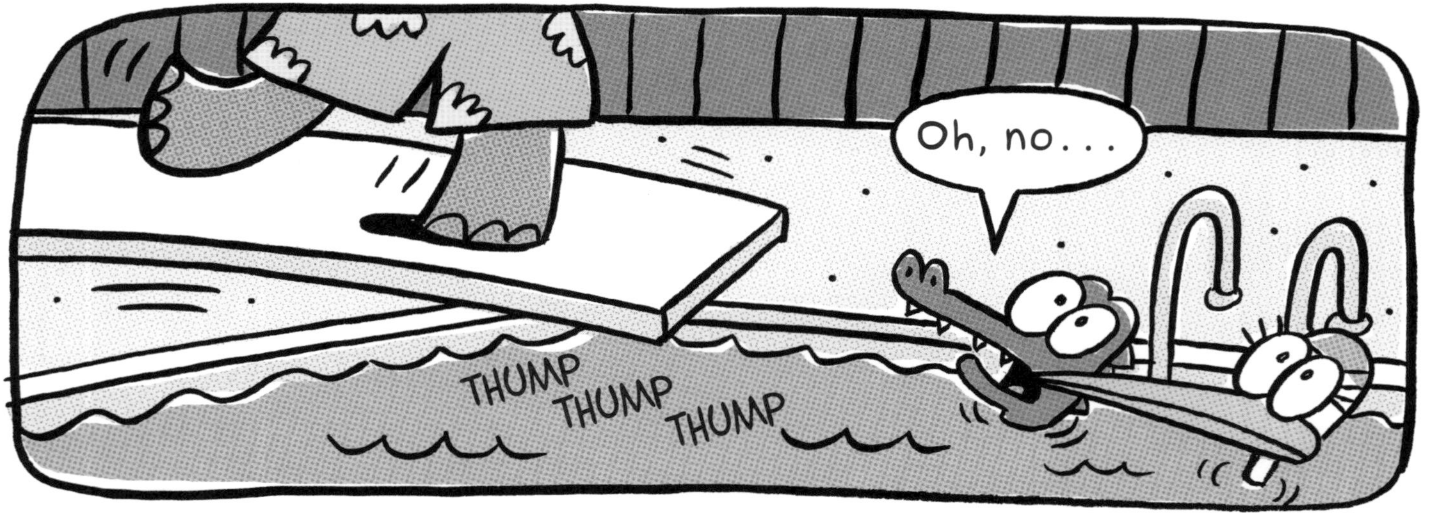
Oh, no. . .
THUMP
THUMP
THUMP

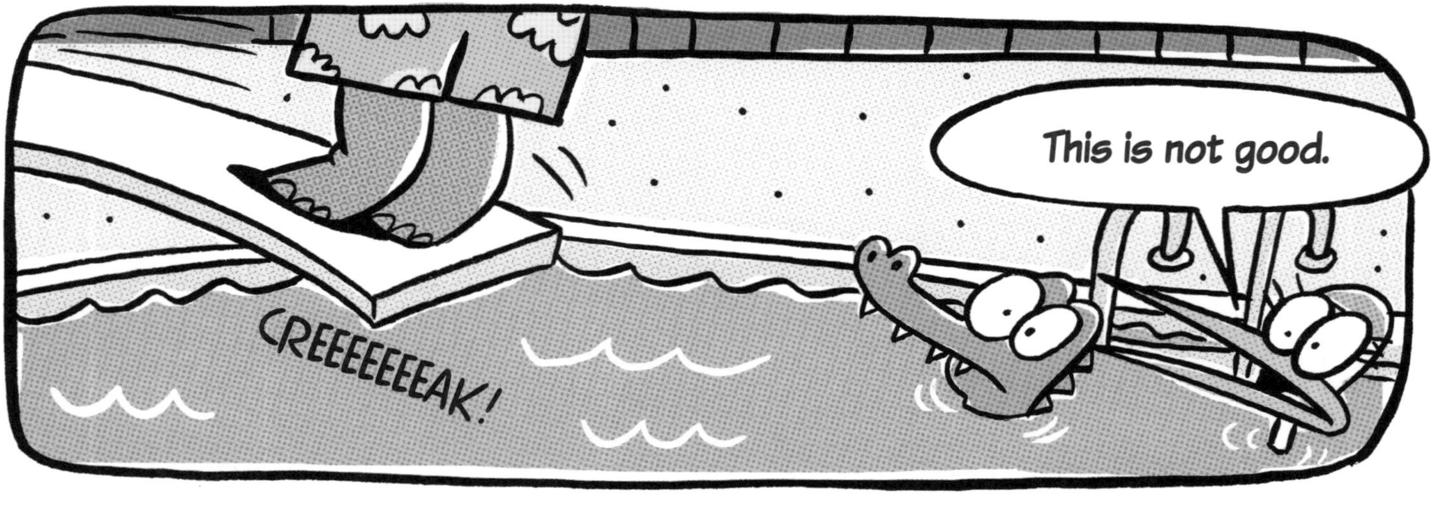
This is not good.
CREEEEEEEEAK!

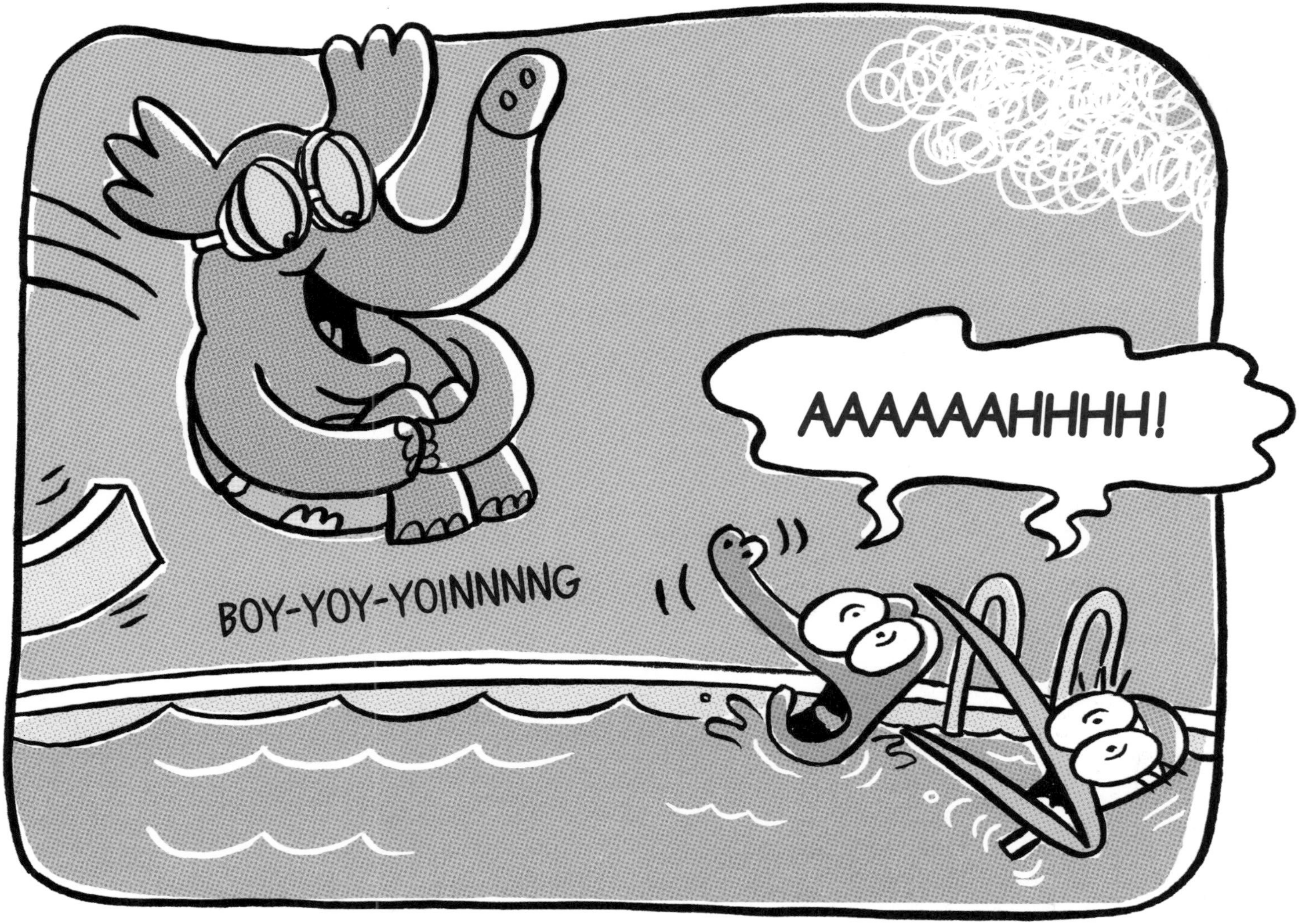
BOY-YOY-YOINNNNG
AAAAAAHHHH!

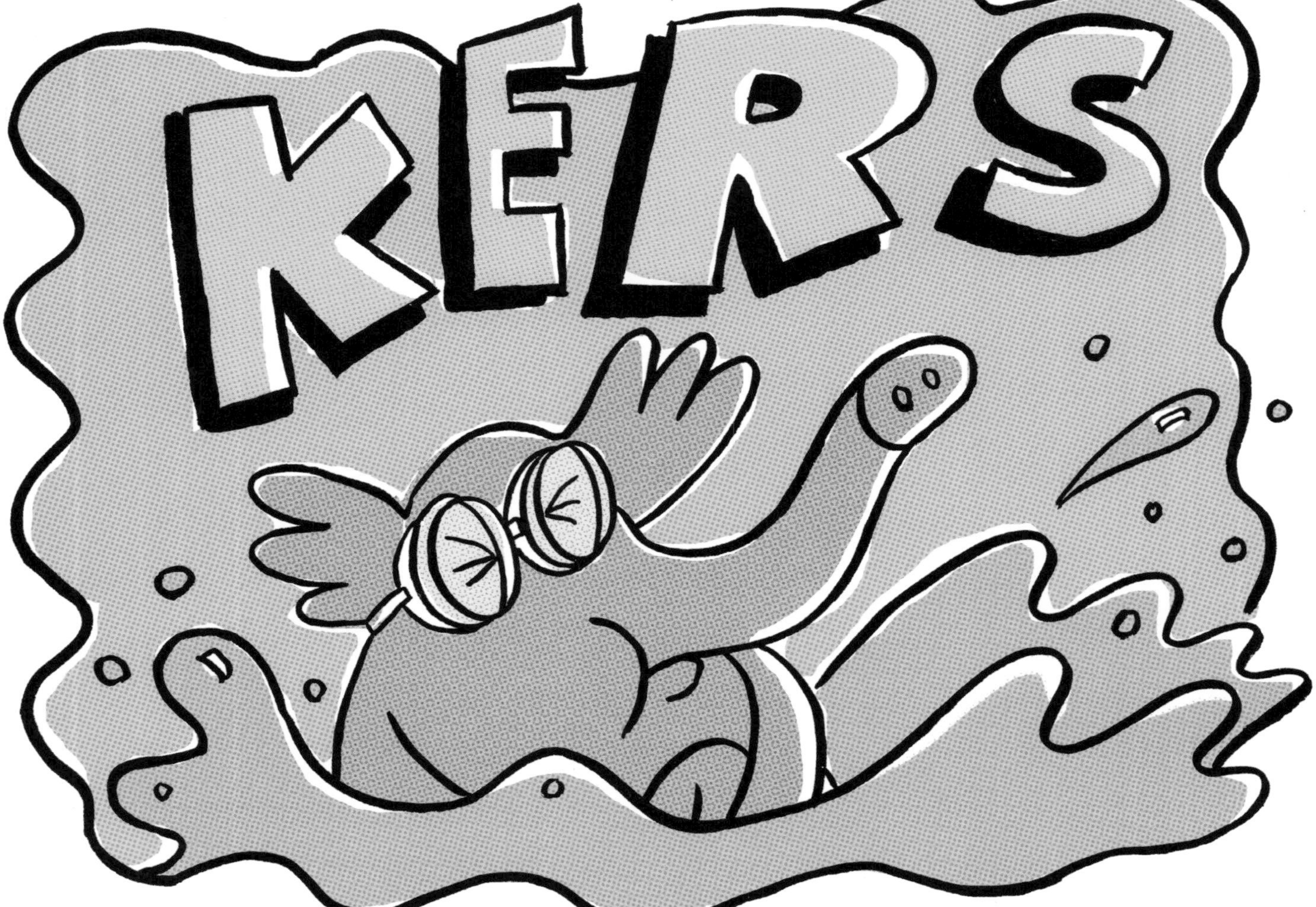
KERS

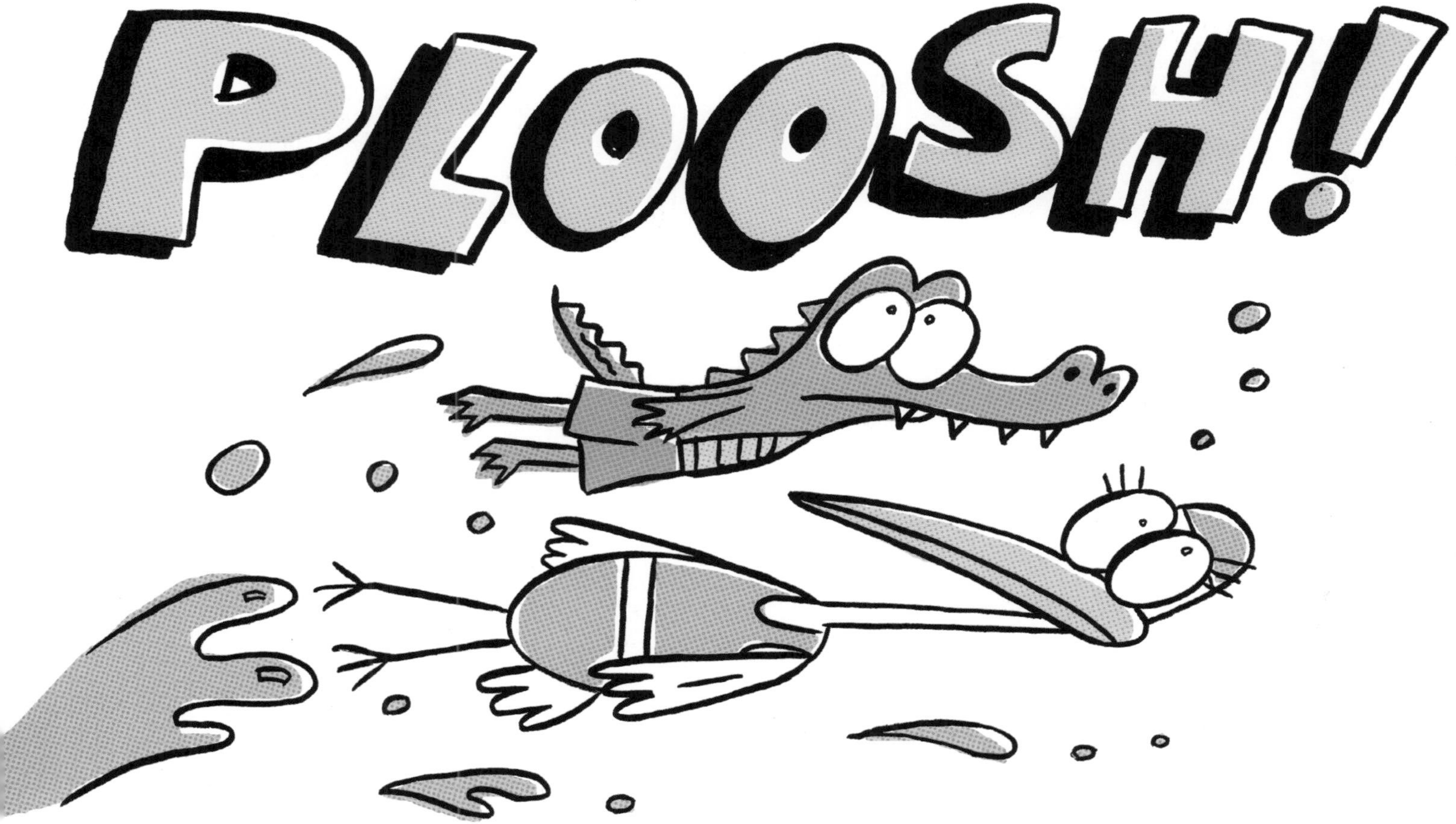
PLOOSH!

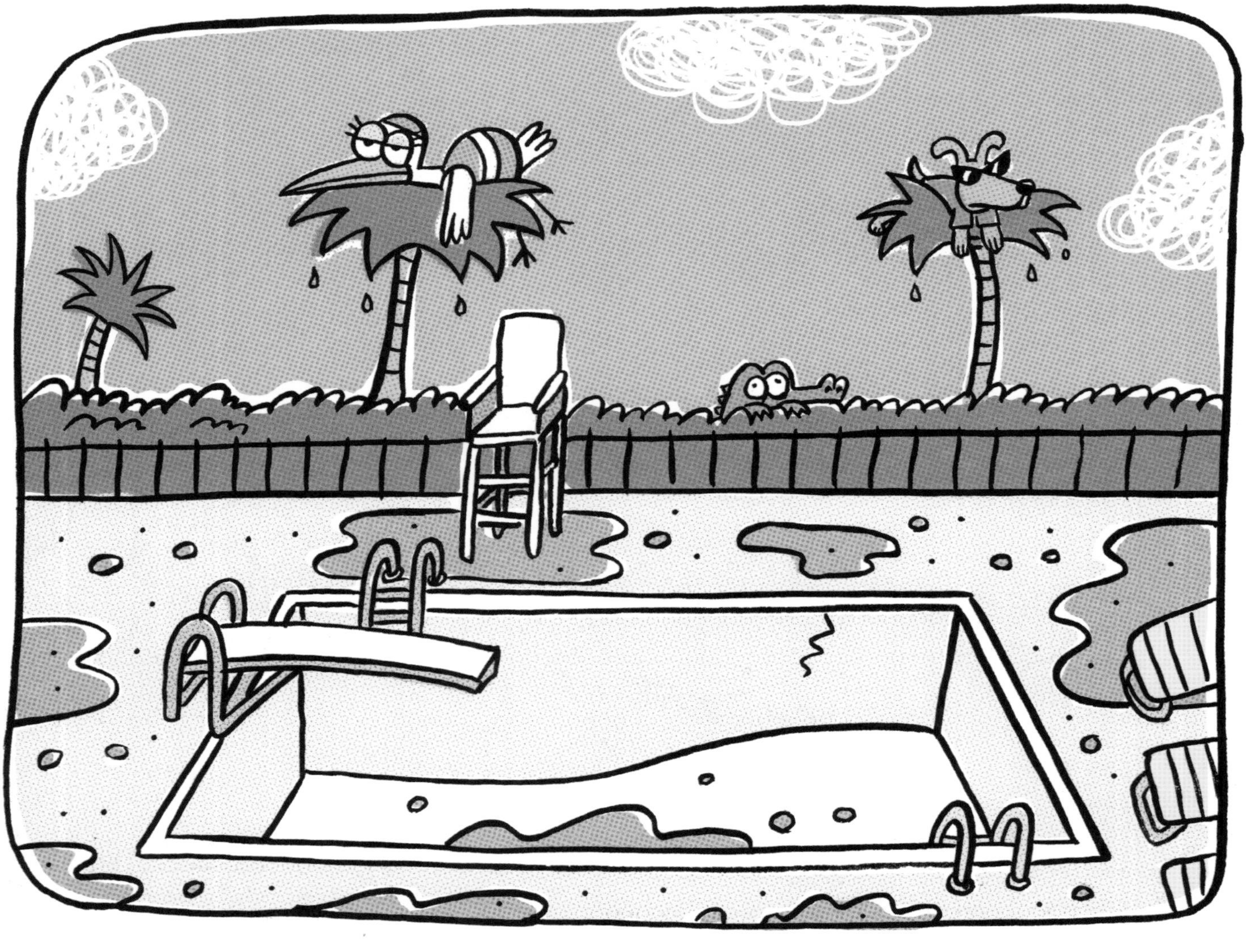

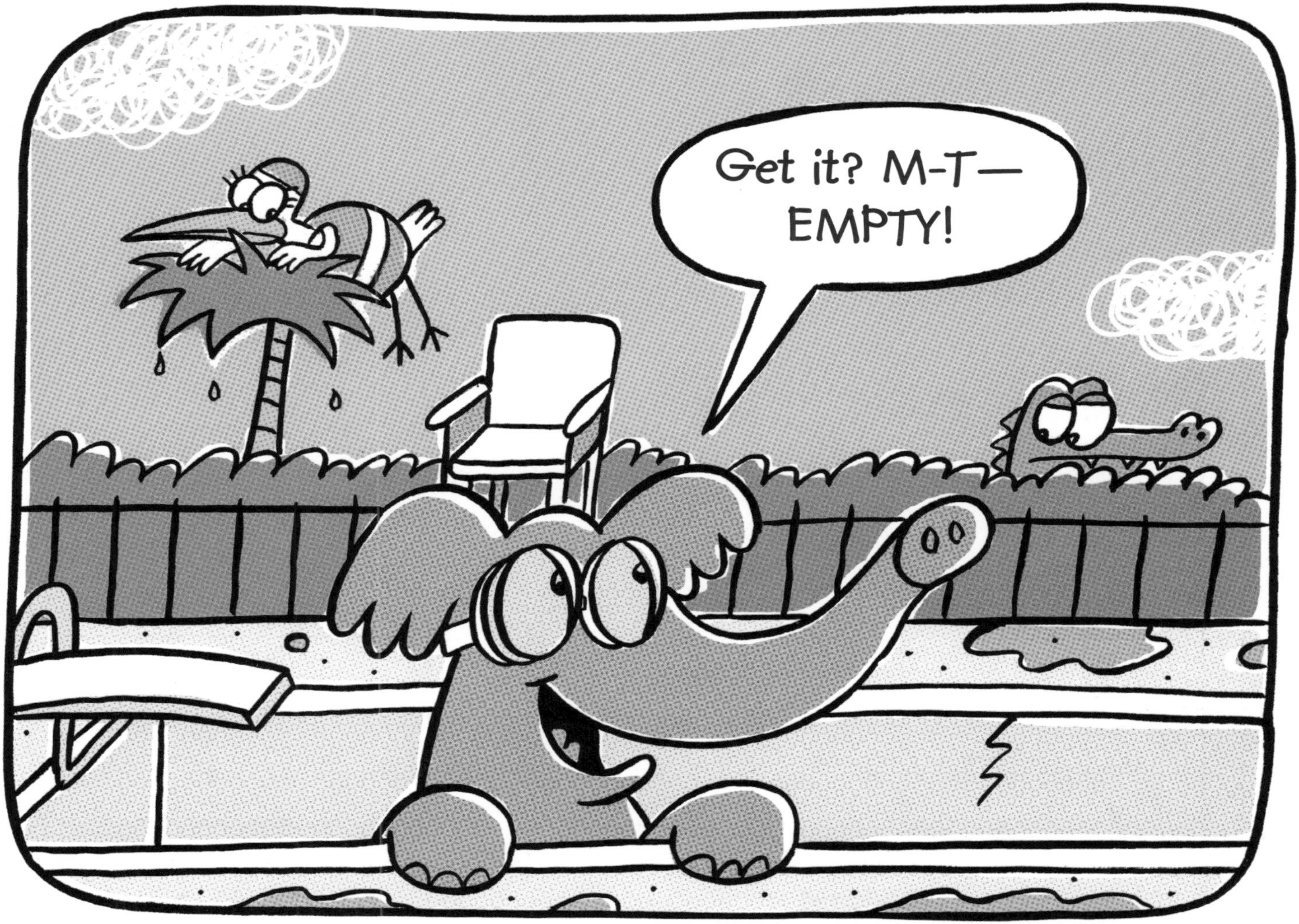
Get it? M-T—
EMPTY!

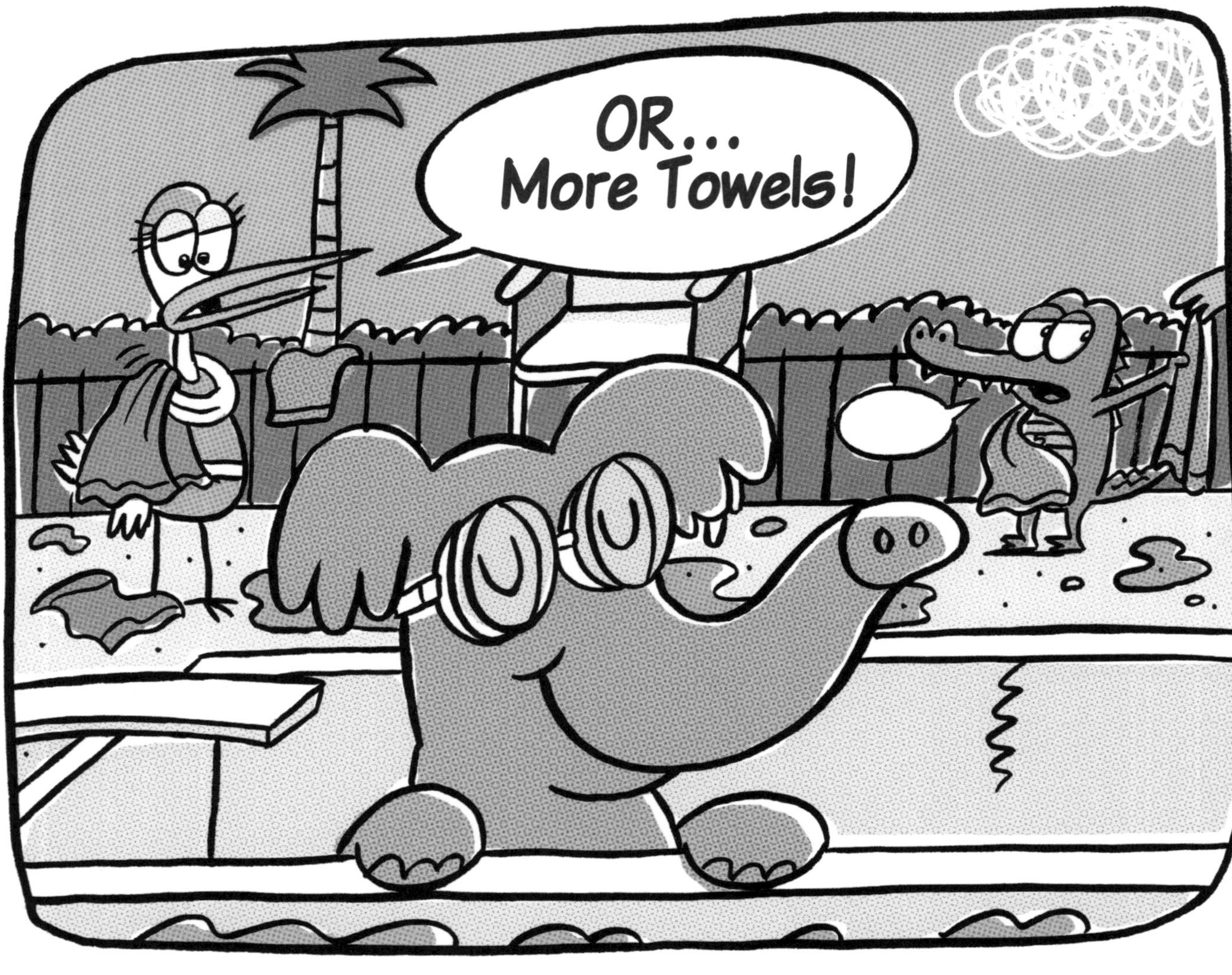
OR...
More Towels!

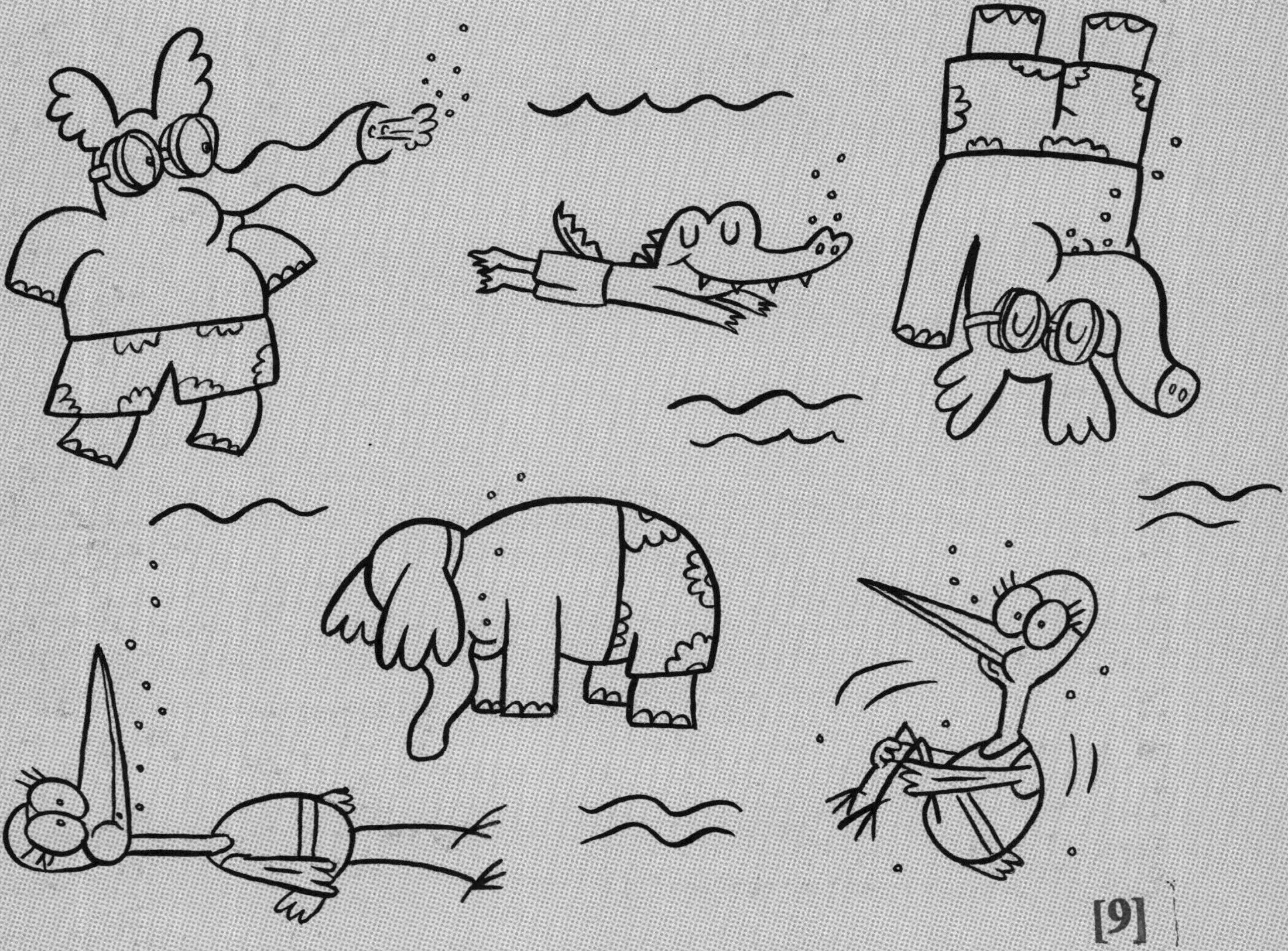